THIS MESS

ne gray rainy afternoon, Daddy stood in the middle of the living room with his hands on his hips and a frown on his face.
"Something has to be done about this mess!" he said.
"I'm going to make some spaghetti sauce and I want you kids to see if you can make this room look better."

And with that, he went to the kitchen and began banging his pots.

Little Salvatore stood on the back of the sofa and surveyed the room through his spyglass. "Hm," he said. "Now what can we do to make this room look better?"

Sophia got up and put all the **BLOCKS** away in the toy chest. "There," said Sophia. "*That's* better," and she sat down.

Elizabeth asked, "What can *I* do to make this room look better?" She thought and she thought, and then she folded the newspapers neatly and took a bow.

"Now you, Salvatore," said Elizabeth. "What can *you* do to make this room look better?" Salvatore turned the lampshade

upside down.

Sophia thought a minute. "What can *I* do to make this room look better?" Then she put all the books in the bookcase in order,
all the **blue** books together,
all the **red** books together,
all the yellow books together.

"Now me! Now me!" Elizabeth said. "What can *I* do to make this room look better?" And she filled the fireplace with shiny blue **balloons**.

Salvatore shouted, "I know what *I* can do to make this room look better," and he took the 𝓯𝓵𝓸𝔀𝓮𝓻𝓼 from the vase and stuck them all over the rocking chair.

Sophia started to smile. "Now what can I do?
What can I *really* do to make this room look better?"
All of a sudden, she started to

> pile
>
> the
>
> sofa
>
> cushions

in a big mountain in the middle of the room, and when
she was done, she sat on them.

"I know what *I* can do to make this room look better," Elizabeth said next. "I'll just move this old window."

And so she **pushed** and **shoved** the window until it looked out on the sun that was beginning to shine through the clouds.

Then it was Salvatore's turn again. "What can I do to make this room look better?" Standing on the Oriental rug, the one with the fringe, he closed his eyes and made it rise up in the air and hover over the sofa.

Sophia and Elizabeth applauded. "What can we do
to make this room look better?" Sophia exclaimed. Then she
sat on the rocking chair, the one with the flowers,
and she made it float to the ceiling.

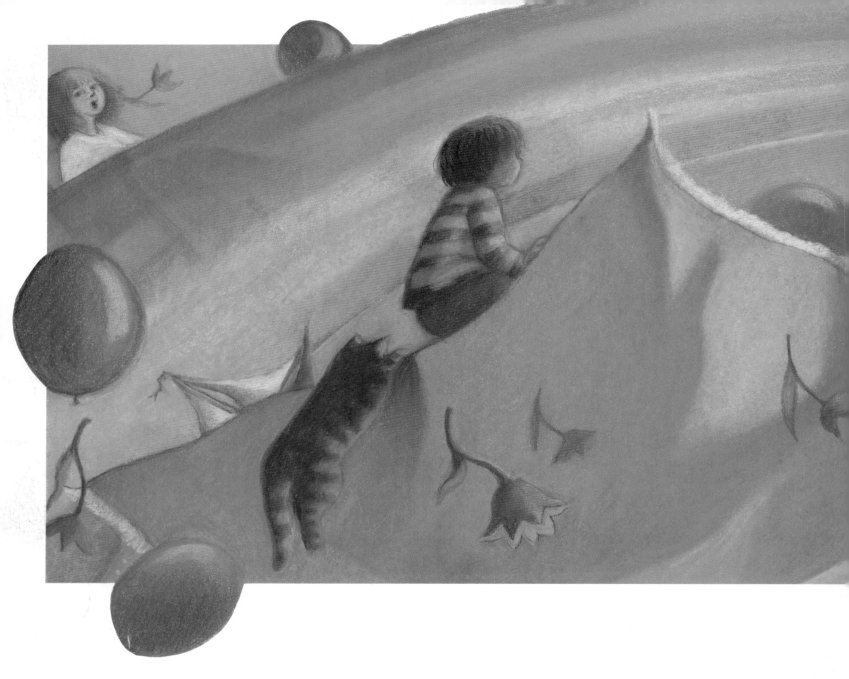

Elizabeth closed her eyes and concentrated. "What can I do?
What can I do to make this room look better?" She opened her eyes,
and with one sweep of her arm . . .

. . . she threw a glimmering **rainbow** across the ceiling.

"How are you doing in there?" Daddy called from the kitchen.

"We're almost done," they answered.

Salvatore was the last to go. Very quietly he asked,
"What can I do to make this room look better?"
The girls waited and watched until, using his flying carpet to
stand on, Salvatore lifted the ceiling, and with one mighty
shove he pushed it off the walls and birds flew around and
the sun shone in on their wonderful room.

Daddy came and stood in the doorway.
"Amazing!" he said. "Amazing, and much,
much better!"

THIS MESS

Pam Conrad
Illustrated by Elizabeth Sayles

Hyperion Books for Children
New York

Printed in Hong Kong by South China Printing Company (1988) Ltd.

First Edition

1 3 5 7 9 10 8 6 4 2

The artwork for each picture is prepared using pastel.
This book is set in 14-point Slimbach.

Library of Congress Cataloging-in-Publication Data
Conrad, Pam.
This Mess / Pam Conrad ; illustrated by Elizabeth Sayles.—1st ed.
p.   cm.
Summary: While Daddy makes spaghetti sauce in the kitchen, Elizabeth, Sophia, and
Salvatore clean up the mess in the living room and give it a fantastic appearance.
ISBN 0-7868-0159-X (trade)—ISBN 0-7868-2131-0 (lib. bdg.)
[1. Orderliness—Fiction. 2. Fantasy.] I. Sayles, Elizabeth, ill. II. Title.
PZ7.C76476Th   1998
[E]—dc21   97-28177